D1097922

THE DINOSAUR THAT POOPED A PRINCESS!

CHECK OUT DANNY AND DINOSAUR IN MORE ADVENTURES:

THE DINOSAUR THAT POOPED A PLANET!

THE DINOSAUR THAT POOPED THE PAST!

THE DINOSAUR THAT POOPED THE BED!

THE DINOSAUR THAT POOPED CHRISTMAS!

For Lola —T. F. & D. P.
For Kyle and Codie —G. P.

ALADDIN

An imprint of Simon & Schuster Children's Publishing Division

1230 Avenue of the Americas, New York, New York 10020

This Aladdin hardcover edition May 2022

Copyright © 2018 by Tom Fletcher and Dougie Poynter

Illustrations by Garry Parsons

Originally published in Great Britain in 2018 by Red Fox, an imprint of Penguin Random House Children's, a division of Penguin Random House UK

All rights reserved, including the right of reproduction in whole or in part in any form.

ALADDIN and related logo are registered trademarks of Simon & Schuster, Inc.

For information about special discounts for bulk purchases, please contact

Simon & Schuster Special Sales at 1-866-506-1949 or business@simonandschuster.com.

The Simon & Schuster Speakers Bureau can bring authors to your live event. For more information or to book an event

contact the Simon & Schuster Speakers Bureau at 1-866-248-3049 or visit our website at www.simonspeakers.com.

Series designed by Nina Simoneaux

Jacket designed by Tiara Iandiorio and Ginny Kemmerer

Manufactured in China 0222 SCP

10 9 8 7 6 5 4 3 2 1

Library of Congress Control Number 2021946002

ISBN 9781534489547 (hc)

ISBN 9781534489554 (ebook)

THE DINOSAUR THAT POOPED A PRINCESS!

Tom Fletcher & Dougie Poynter
Illustrated by Garry Parsons

ALADDIN

NEW YORK   LONDON   TORONTO   SYDNEY   NEW DELHI

Once upon a time . . .

Danny was riding his dinosaur steed
  In search of a princess who longed to be freed,
But soon they were lost in Fairy-Tale Land,
  So they asked for directions from Gingerbread Man.

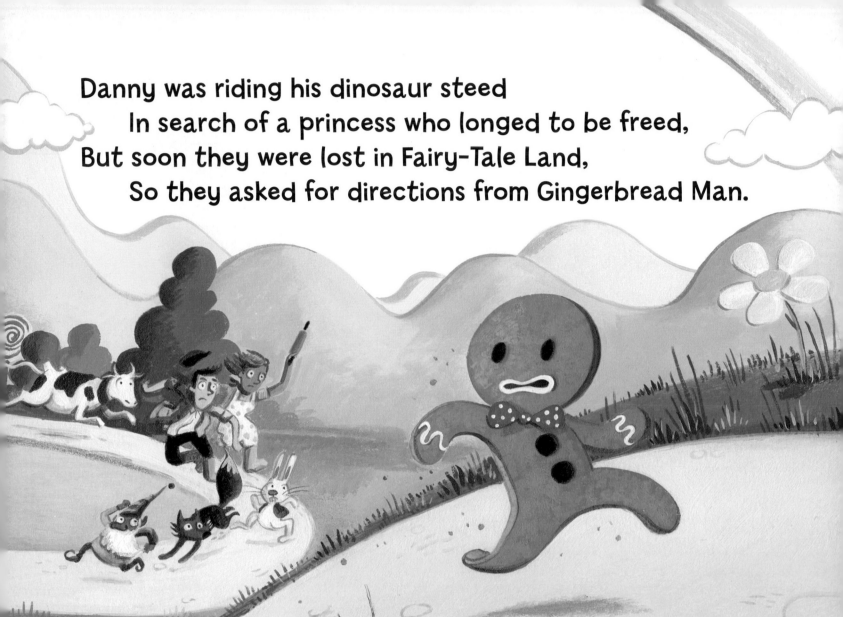

"Gingerbread Man, oh, Gingerbread Man,
  Show us the way we should go, if you can."

Gingerbread Man scratched his gingerbread head.
   He thought for a moment and then suddenly said:

"I cannot remember!
   My brain's made of dough.
But go ask the Three Little Pigs—
   They might know!"

Then as they set off down the yellow brick track,
Dinosaur ate up that gingerbread snack!

They soon came across the Three Little Pigs,
    Rebuilding their houses of brick, straw, and twigs.
"Three Little Pigs, oh, Three Little Pigs,
    Princess needs help—do you know where she is?"

The Three Little Pigs made
a little pig huddle,
But they couldn't agree—
they were all in a muddle.

"She's this way! She's that way!
    She's down there!" they said.
"Why don't you go ask
    Prince Charming instead?"

But while Danny worked out which road should be taken,
The pigs smelled like bacon—so Dinosaur ate them!

They soon
found the prince
at the grand palace ball.
He made everyone laugh
in that royal-sized hall.

"Prince Charming, oh,
Prince Charming, Sir,
The princess needs help,
and we can't find her."

He gazed in the mirror that hung on the wall.
Then the prince swooshed his hair and announced to them all:

He wrote down the way they should go on a scroll . . .

Before Dinosaur swallowed that charming prince whole.

With Prince Charming's directions they started their quest . . .

Passed the troll on the bridge

and the rotten orcs' nest.

Tippy-toed
past the dragon,
asleep on
its gold,

Fooled the witch,
easy-peasy—
in a pot full of
mold.

Tamed the wolf in the wood,

Swam the sea of quicksand,

Climbed the beanstalk
and high-fived the
giant's huge hand.

But with Danny
so focused on
saving the maiden,

How was he to know
that his noble steed
ate them?

"There it is! There it is!"
Danny called to his steed.
"It shan't be long now
till the princess is freed!"

"Princess, oh, Princess,
Please let down your hair!
We've come here to save you,
But can't find the stairs!"

Danny shouted
and called,
but there came
no reply . . .

So he sat on
the ground,

and he started to cry.

Just then an idea pinged in Dinosaur's head:
Perhaps they could fly up the tower instead!

With fairy-tale creatures deep down in its gut,
Its brain made a wish involving its butt.

It knew there was only one thing it could do—
To save the princess it needed to . . .

POO!

Like a giant poo fountain, they shot up the tower,
Giving Fairy-Tale Land a smelly poo shower.

It pooped orcs and trolls
all over the place,
And the prince still looked charming
with poop on his face.

Dino's butt huffed and guffed
as he pooped out the pigs,
Blowing down their new houses
of brick, straw, and twigs.

The giant, the wolf, and the sea of quicksand,
The dragon, its gold, and the gingerbread man.

They flew higher and higher with poop-powered thrust,
And the poop was all sparkly, like brown pixie dust.

They crashed
through the roof
in a mighty
poo mess . . .

Then out of the dust came
one angry princess!

"My bedroom! It used to be pretty and blue.
And now it's all gooey and dripping with poo!
I didn't need saving—my home is this tower.
Now I'll make this mess right with my princess girl power!"

She swished with her wand,
and she clicked her heels too.
And then she sang, "Bibbedy,

Bobbedy,

POO!"

Loads of magic appeared from the wand in her hand . . .

And the
poop disappeared
from Fairy-Tale Land!

"We're sorry," Dan said, "for the way we behaved.
Now we know not all princesses need to be saved!"

This story is over. The sun is descending.
But wait! There's a twist to this fairy-tale ending . . .

Because Dino had nothing better to do,
It swallowed the princess and pooped her out too!